# The Tree In Their Backyard

EILEEN DISTASIO-CLARK

*With Great Love and Appreciation to Those Who Have and Do Bless My Life.*

## *My Family:*

*Joseph DeStasio Sr. & Miriam Lucille Baragone DeStasio, My Late Parents.*

*Andrea Jean DeStasio McIntosh, My Older Sister and Their Families.*

*Joseph DeStasio Jr., My Younger and Only Brother and Their Families.*

*Donna Marie DeStasio Wagner, My Younger Sister and Their Families.*

## *My Children:*

*Eileen, Rebekah, Rachel, S. Michael,*

*Jennifer, Sharon, Tara, Stephanie,*

*Apryll, Mikaelah, & M. Trevor*

*and THEIR Families!!*

# ACKNOWLEDGEMENTS

First and foremost, I express, deeply, my sincere gratitude to our Heavenly Father for blessing me with the gift and talent of writing! I know I could not do what I do without His assistance.

I also want to acknowledge and express gratitude to the members of my birth family—Joseph Sr., Miriam, Andrea, Joseph Junior, and Donna. All the experiences of my childhood years, experiences that taught me so very much and enabled me to reveal my true self to myself, came about through my experiences and relationships with them.

And, of course, it goes without saying, but I will say it anyway: I also want to acknowledge and note my gratitude to my children, Eileen, Rebekah, Rachel, S. Michael, Jennifer, Sharon, Tara, Stephanie, Apryll, Mikaelah, and M. Trevor, and their families! Through multiple things they said to me, over multiple years, I finally came to the realization that Heavenly Father gave me the gift of writing and opened the doors to these experiences because He knew that by sharing them with others, others could feel His love too.

And He definitely wants us all to know that He, Heavenly Father, Heavenly Mother, and Jehovah truly do loves us!!!

# INTRODUCTION

There are sixteen books in this series, which I refer to as *"The Ellie Series."* All of the characters in these stories portray real people from my life. The main characters depict the members of my family: Daddy is my daddy; Mommy is my mommy; Jeannie is my older sister; Junior is my brother; Maria is my younger sister, and Ellie is me. Now, those are not our actual first names, but they do reference us.

The first story in the series presents our Heavenly Father's Plan of Salvation and takes place in the Pre-Earth World. Now, of course, because we all—when we were born—received what is known as The Veil of Forgetfulness, I do not actually remember everything from or about the Pre-Earth World, but I do know about and understand it from much study and worship as a member of The Church of Jesus Christ of Latter-Day Saints, and memories restored to me through the Holy Spirit. So, from this story there is much truth to be learned.

The last story in the series is set in the Post-Mortal World, and presents a depiction of what happens to us after this life. Again, because I have not gone there yet, I cannot say I 'remember' this. But, I have also learned about the Post-Mortal World from much study and worship as a member of The Church of Jesus Christ of Latter-Day Saints.

All of the other stories are based on true events from my life; events that actually occurred when and how they are depicted in these stories. I chose these events because they are among the many occurrences in my life that presented—or revealed that which I already knew without having to be taught—Principles of Eternal Truths.

Also, I chose these events as the settings for my stories because they depict wonderful learning moments from my childhood and adolescent years, lessons that have blessed and benefited me throughout the whole of my life and will forever continue to do so. Also, through these great truths and their consequences in my life, I have been able to share them with many others, whose lives have also been blessed by them.

So, please, read and enjoy, then care and share the messages and stories with others!!

Now, there are also a couple of things you can look for:

In each story, the title of the previous story is presented in *italicized* form, the title of the next story is presented in *Capitalized Italicized* form, and the title of the story being read is presented in **emboldened** form.

Also, every story has at least one word that is uncommon or 'created.'

So, as you read, search, find, and have fun!

# THE TREE IN THEIR BACKYARD

When Ellie was a little girl, a small baby, she lived in a pretty little big house, with a pretty big little backyard. There was a really neat hopscotch diagram on the pavement behind the house, that Daddy had painted for them, and a really fun swing set on the grass in front of the garage. But the best part of their yard, at least in Ellie's mind, was their tree—a really, really, really... okay, you get the idea, a really tall Catalpa tree.

Ellie liked to sit under the tree; she even tried to climb up into the tree. She liked to collect the 'elephant ear' leaves and the giant 'bean sticks' when they fell off the tree. Oh, and when the 'bean sticks' fell off the tree, Ellie would try to pull them open. Yes, she loved their Catalpa tree, but there were also things about the Catalpa that Ellie wanted to know.

Now, that was no surprise. Nope, there was no question at all! It was far too obvious for anyone to even begin to try to wonder! That fact was more than definitely overly easy to see!

'What is she talking about?' You may be asking yourself. 'What does all that have to do with the Catalpa tree?'

Well, I will tell you; this is what I am talking about. Ellie! Ellie Stations!! She was, and is, a truly natural learner! In fact, it seemed that there were some things that Ellie just knew! How? No one knew, but it sure was apparent that she did. And it also was quite obvious that she was born with a very well-developed sense of inquisition.

'Wait! What is that?' You are now probably wondering. Well, that—said another way—is this. Ellie was incredibly curious about everything. And, she did not stop at just wondering about things; she asked Daddy and Mommy endless questions about them and listened intently to every answer they gave her. In fact, she listened to everything that anyone said about anything.

She even looked at books about all kinds of things, even before she could read, or read very well. You see, she seemed to be able to learn quite a bit just by looking at the pictures. Oh, and by the way, this curiosity of hers, the eagerness that inspired and motivated her to look, to listen, and to learn, never faded; as she grew, so did it!

Yes! Yes indeed. Ellie definitely did, and still does, like to learn about everything. So, it was no wonder that when Jeannie, her sister, who was seven years old, and Ellie played together in their yard, Ellie would ask Jeannie questions about the Catalpa, but the only answer she got from Jeannie was, "I don't know. Go ask Daddy."

When she gave Junior, her two-year-old, rides around the yard, either on her tricycle or in their wagon, she did not even try to ask him because she knew he would not know either. When she 'played' with Maria, her one-year-old baby sister, she did not even think about the tree. Instead, she focused on doing silly things that would make Maria laugh. So, sadly, Ellie could not seem to answer her own questions like, why the top branches moved so much!

When Ellie looked up, trying to see the top of the tree, and saw those branches moving, swaying, in a pleasant kind of way, she thought for sure that the tree went all the way to Heaven and that there were angels sitting on the top branches, swaying them the same way that Ellie swung the swings when she sat on them. One day, she decided she was going to climb the tree, to say hello to the angels, and ask them why they moved the branches like that. So, up she started.

Well, at least, she tried to start up the tree but, being only five years old, and quite small, smaller than all the other five-year-old kids she knew, it did not take her long to realize that she was not yet big enough to climb their Catalpa. After all, the trunk was too big, really big, bigger than the moon, and the lowest branches were too high, really high, higher than her Uncle Tom, who was sixteen feet tall. (That was what she thought when she was a little girl, a very little girl. Actually, her Uncle Tom was only six feet tall, but that was still quite tall for an Italian.)

Anyway, she sat down beneath the tree, wondering, 'How did this tree get to be so tall?' She thought for a moment, or two, or three, or… okay, you know what I am saying, she thought, *Maybe the angels stretched it so they could sit up there and keep an eye on me.* After all, Mommy was always saying, "Ellie, I need eyes on the back of my head to keep track of you."

*But maybe,* she thought instead, *it was just born that way.* She had never seen a little tree; it was just that her Catalpa tree was so much bigger than all the other trees.

While Ellie was sitting there thinking, Daddy got home from work. After greeting Mommy with a great big little hug and a kiss, he said hello to Jeannie and asked her about her day. Then, he picked up Junior and tossed him up and down like a basketball a few times, before holding Maria, the baby, for a little bit. Then, knowing that Ellie would be in the backyard, he headed out there to say hello to her too, and to see what she was doing. Of course, he knew exactly where to find her because he knew how much she loved sitting under her favourite Catalpa tree.

As he walked across the hopscotch and stepped onto the grass, he called to Ellie, "How is my little girl, my very little girl?"

Hearing Daddy's voice, and with all the energy of a dolphin leaping out of the water, Ellie jumped up, spun around, ran the couple of feet that was between them, leaped into his arms, and gave him a great big 'little hug.' Then, to answer his question, as he returned a great big 'little hug,' she said, "Well, I am confuzzled."

"Really," he asked with a smile on his face, as they both sat down under the tree and leaned against its trunk, "why are you confuzzled?"

"Because," she explained, "I cannot figure out how Catalpa got to be so big; was it born that way?"

"Born that way?" Daddy laughed. "No, it was not born that way." Then, with the intent to answer her question in a way that would make sense to a five-year-old, he stood up, reached up to the lowest branch, and pulled a 'bean stick' off of the tree.

***Side Note:** That was what Ellie, when she was a little, a very little girl, called them. They were really just long, really long, longer than Pinocchio's nose, seedpods, about as long as a ruler, or almost two of them. Now, back to Daddy and the seedpod. ***

After pulling a bean stick off of the tree, he sat down beside Ellie, peeled the string off, opened the pod, and took out a seed. "This is how big it was when it was born," he said.

Ellie's eyes popped, like corn kernels in hot butter! Her jaw dropped, like a yo-yo out of an open hand! It was amazing, utterly amazing! It was incredible, totally incredible!! It was unbelievable, downright unbelievable!!! Yes, it was just too much for a little girl like Ellie, a very little girl like Ellie, to make sense of! Why, that seed was no bigger than the tip of Daddy's baby finger, which was actually pretty big for a seed, but Ellie did not know that.

"Wait a minute, Daddy," Ellie exclaimed, "how could a seed that little," Ellie pointed to the seed, "become a tree this big?!" Ellie pointed up to Catalpa. Daddy laughed, and then settled back against the big, really big, bigger than the moon, trunk of Catalpa, and told Ellie all about how their Catalpa grew.

"Once upon... hmmmm... an unknown time ago," Daddy began, in story-telling mode, "there was a little Catalpa seed, about that size," Daddy handed the seed to Ellie, "that was drifting lazily on the waves of a warm spring breeze. It ran up and down hills, jumped over rivers and brooks, spun around houses, past cars, and under bridges, and danced through open windows and doors, until finally, it came to rest... right here," Daddy pointed to the ground beneath the tree, right next to the spot where Ellie was sitting. "As with all things on the ground," Daddy said, "it got stepped on."

"Oh, Daddy," Ellie asked sadly, "who would step on a Catalpa seed?"

"Well," Daddy replied, somewhat amused, "little girls, very little girls, like you."

Ellie was shocked. "Not me!" she exclaimed. "I would never step on a Catalpa seed!"

"And little boys," Daddy continued, "very little boys, like me."

Ellie was amazed. "Daddy," she said, "you are not a little boy."

"Nooo, not now," he said, "but I was, when the seed that grew this tree," he pointed to their Catalpa, "was lying on the ground."

Now Ellie was both shocked and amazed. "Daddy," she said, "that was a long, really long, longer than Sleeping Beauty's nap, time ago."

"Hmmmm, was it now?" Daddy asked, with a curious look on his face, but he continued, "Well, it does take a long, long, really long, longer than Sleeping Beauty's nap, time for a seed this small to grow into a tall, tall, really tall, taller than your Uncle Tom, tree."

"Ooohh," Ellie said thoughtfully, "I think that is true."

"Yes, it is," Daddy said, "but it takes more than just time. It was dark in the ground, so the seed had to break out of its shell and push up through the dirt before it could really begin to grow."

"Yeah," Ellie said thoughtfully, "it probably did not like being in the ground. It is cold, and dark, and dirty down there."

"Yes, it is," Daddy agreed, and then continued with, "but once it popped up, out of the dirt, it began to spread out, well, at least up. And up it went, through the rain, when it rained, through the sunshine, when the sun shined, and through the wind, when the wind, winded. It just kept going up."

"Yeah, up and up and up." Ellie sighed as she looked up at the tree with Daddy. "I love my Catalpa tree!" she said softly.

Daddy smiled as he looked up at the tree with Ellie. He, too, liked their Catalpa tree. It was tall and stately, broad and bountiful, and it was beautiful!!

As if hearing Daddy's thoughts, Ellie softly repeated, "Pretty, pretty, pretty!" Then, to Daddy she said, "I love the big, really big, bigger than an elephant's ears, leaves that grow on it. How big are they, Daddy?"

"Oh, about as long as a big ruler and as wide as a small one," Daddy said.

"They look like green hearts," Ellie told him, then asked, "Did you know that?"

"Yes," he said, "I believe I told you that."

"Oh, yeah," Ellie replied shyly and with an innocent smile, "and I love the pretty, really pretty, prettier than church windows' flowers. They remind me of Grandma's Sunday china, especially the sugar bowl, the one that has curls on the top."

Daddy smiled even bigger. "Yes," he said, "the one that has curls on the top."

Then, thoughtfully, Ellie asked, "When did Catalpa get its flowers?"

Daddy thought for a moment, then said, "When it was about six or seven years old."

"What?" Ellie responded, "Why did it take so long?"

"It had to get its seedpods first," Daddy explained.

"When did it get those?" Ellie asked.

"When it was about five or six years old," Daddy said. Now, I guess he could see that Ellie was surprised because, before she could say anything else, he said, "Even when Catalpa was a baby tree, she was strong, really strong, stronger than the bull on Old Don's farm. Nothing could stop her from growing. The winter snows did not; even the icy rains could not bend her branches. But, before she could grow the seedpods and blossoms, she had to be bigger than big and stronger than strong. So, she just kept growing. But...," he continued, "even while she was waiting for her seedpods and blossoms, she still helped the birds."

"How did she do that?" Ellie asked.

"Because she is so tall, and she has lots of nice, big leaves, the birds were safe sitting on her branches and building their nests there," Daddy explained. "And," he added, "every year, she gave us nice, cool shade with those big, big, really big, bigger than elephant's ears, green heart-shaped leaves."

"...even when the Catty wormblies ate them?" Ellie asked. (That was what she called the worms that they sometimes found on the leaves.)

"...even when the Catty wormblies ate them," Daddy said. "In fact, when the Catalpa worms munched and nibbled on her old leaves, she just grew new ones, faster than they could finish their dinner. So, you see, once Catalpa's seed popped through the dirt, she just kept growing up, and up, and up, until she was all the way up there."

Daddy looked up. Ellie looked up. Ellie was quiet for a moment, then, quizzically, she asked, "How long did it take to get up there?"

"Oh," Daddy thought for a moment, then said, "about twenty years."

"WHAT?!" Ellie exclaimed. "Why did she grow so slow?"

"The Catalpa tree is actually a fast-growing tree," Daddy said. "But it takes a long time to get that tall."

"How tall, is that tall?" Ellie asked.

"Taller than your Uncle Tom," Daddy replied in a teasing tone. They both laughed, and then Daddy said, "That tall is a bit more than fifty feet, maybe sixty. And, Ellie, this one is a little Catalpa, a very little Catalpa. Some Catalpas are seventy-five or eighty feet tall, and some are hundred feet or more."

"Woooow," Ellie said, "I think I cannot think of anything to say."

"Wow!" Daddy replied, "That never happens."

Daddy and Ellie laughed together, shared a pretty big 'little hug,' then, again, leaned back against the Catalpa, looking up into the highest branches, where, as I said before, Ellie was sure the angels sat and watched them.

After a moment or two, or three, or maybe four, Ellie leaned against Daddy's arm and quietly sighed, a pleasant sigh. "Daddy," she said, "I am so happy that we have a Catalpa tree."

"Ellie," Daddy said back to her, "I am so happy that you are so happy that we have a Catalpa tree! But I am also curious; why does it make you so happy?"

"'Cause," Ellie began to explain as she sat up, moved in front of Daddy, and looked at him, "it is soooooo pretty! I like Catalpa's twisty…" Ellie paused, looked at the tree, then, as she patted the trunk of the tree, she asked, "What is this?"

"It is Catalpa's trunk," Daddy answered.

Ellie looked at him with a confused expression. After a few moments, her confusion apparently transformed into delight, with a great big smile and the sound of playful excitement in her voice, she said, "Oh! So, Catalpa really is an elephant!"

"What?" Daddy asked, a little confused.

"You said this is a trunk," Ellie answered with a hint of teasing amusement. "And these," she continued as she got up, stepped on the big rock that was beside the tree, and picked a leaf off of the tip of the lowest branch, "look like elephant ears. Soooo, since Catalpa has a trunk and elephant ears, she must be an elephant!"

Ellie began laughing and, of course, Daddy joined in! How could he not?! Only Ellie would come up with a conclusion like that, well, maybe not only Ellie, but for someone so young, she sure was good at it! Yep! Fun and funny! That was Ellie! You always had to expect the unexpected from her. But then again, with her, the unexpected was the expected, as long as it was good! And that was what she liked best about their Catalpa.

'Huh?' you are probably thinking. 'How does that connect?

Well, I will tell you; that connects like this.

After tossing the leaf onto the ground, Ellie sat back down beside Daddy, leaned against him, and wrapped her arms around his arm, then looked up again at Catalpa's highest branches, which, as they always did, were swaying back and forth, and forth and back, and back and fo... well, you get the idea. Anyway, as Ellie watched them, she began to hum.

Then, seeing that Daddy was watching them too, she finished her explanation as to why she liked their Catalpa so much.

"I like Catalpa's big, really big, bigger than the moon, twisty trunk," she began. "I like Catalpa's 'elephant ear' leaves that look like green hearts," she continued. "I like Catalpa's long, really long, longer than Pinocchio's nose 'bean sticks.' I like Catalpa's pretty, really pretty, prettier than church windows flowers," she added. "But, best of all," Ellie paused for a moment, watching the highest branches sway, then said, "I like the angels who sit up there, in Catalpa's top branches." With a loving kind of sigh and a tight hug to Daddy's arm, she concluded with, "They make me happy!"

So serious did Ellie's words sound that Daddy had to look at her to see what her expression was saying. There was not a hint of jest in her eyes, not a suggestion of teasing in her smile; nope, nothing anywhere on her face that evidenced anything other than complete seriousness!

"Ellie," Daddy asked, in a tone that was just as serious as Ellie's words and expressions, "why do you think there are angels up there? Do you really believe that?"

"Yes, Daddy, I do," Ellie replied quietly, but with a sincerity that expressed the idea that she actually knew, had knowledge that there were angels on the top branches, and did not just believe, had a hope, that there were.

"But Angels live in heaven, Ellie," Daddy said, instructively.

"I know, Daddy," Ellie said, "you told me that before. But Daddy, God sends them here too, to help us. He would do that for us. Right?" Then after a short, quiet pause, Ellie continued with, "Remember when I wanted to do summer catechism with Jeannie last year, and Sister Mary and Sister Theresa said I could not because I was only four years old and that was too young? I was so sad, so when we got home, I went to my room to get my horsey, and then I came out here to Catalpa. I sat down and started moving back and forth while I was talking to *my horsey, my horsey, my horsey*. But when I saw the branches up there moving, I knew the angels were there, so I told them how much I had liked saying the Rosary prayers with Jeannie, and how much I loved the stories that Sister Mary had told us about Jesus. I told them that I even had fun playing the games with the other kids at recess. But then, I cried and told them how sad I was that I could not go back." After a second short, quiet pause, Ellie continued with, "Then, when I looked up, I saw the branches moving, and Daddy, that was when I did not feel bad anymore. The angels helped me feel better."

Daddy thought for a moment. He recalled some of the wonderful, truly miraculous experiences he and his family had lived through during his growing-up years. He remembered many things that had happened that saved lives, some of which he had participated in. He thought about the numerous unexplainable occurrences that he had witnessed as a soldier during World War II by which he and his comrades and been protected and guided. He realized that many, if not all, of those things could not have occurred without the help of angels. He thought about times when things were lost, like *The Ring* that his dad had given to his mom, and were only found because they simply appeared where they had not been when they searched for them. They had all agreed that an Angel must have found it for them. He also thought about Bible stories, in which angels did visit, instruct, and help people, and he silently asked himself, 'If God sent angels then, why not now?'

After a moment, or two, or thre... well, you know. Daddy said softly, "Ellie, you are right!" He picked her up, sat her on his lap, and gave her another pretty big 'little hug,' only that time, it was a pretty big, 'BIG hug.' Then he said, with humble pride and gratitude, "Ellie, I am so happy to see that you really are one truly spiritual little lady. And I know you must be! How else could you know that there really are angels sitting up there, on Catalpa's highest branches?"

Ellie smiled at Daddy, gave him a pretty big 'little hug' as big as Ellie could muster and asked, "Can I go up and see them?"

Now, Daddy was both a bit alarmed and somewhat comforted by her question. He felt alarmed because he knew, without a doubt, that Ellie most definitely would attempt to climb all the way up to the highest branches. But he was also comforted by the knowledge that she was too small to even begin to try to attempt such a climb. Still, what about when she got bigger, or at least older, he was pretty sure, no, not pretty sure, he was absolutely certain she would, as soon as she could, try to climb all the way up to those top branches.

Finally, in reply to her question, with the unspoken hope that she would lose interest in such a quest as she grew older, he said, "Well, Ellie, not now. You are much too small to even begin to climb the Catalpa. Maybe later, when you are bigger, quite a bit bigger, maybe then you can climb to the top of Catalpa and say hello to the Angels who are there."

About the time Daddy was done answering Ellie's question, dinner was ready, and Mommy was calling for everyone to come to the table. So, Daddy stood Ellie up on the ground beside him, pulled himself up, took Ellie's hand in his, and headed for the house. Just before stepping through the doorway, Ellie looked back at the Catalpa tree. As Daddy watched Ellie smile and felt her little shake of excitement, it was quite evident to him that Ellie was truly grateful for the tree in their backyard!

# ABOUT THE AUTHOR

Eileen DiStasio-Clark is the second oldest of four children. She is the mother of eleven children and grandmother to twenty-three grandchildren, to date. As a member of The Church of Jesus Christ of Latter-Day Saints, she serves in various positions, teaching, leading, and ministering to children, youth, and adults. Currently, she is also a Family History Missionary. Eileen established the Pursuit of Excellence Institute of Family Education, a non-profit organization focused on strengthening the family. Presently she holds an AA, a BA, and an MA in Clinical Psychology and is working on the completion of her Doctoral Degree.